A WOODLAND MYSTERY™

The Mad Scientist

A WOODLAND MYSTERY
By Irene Schultz

The Wright Group®

To my grandchildren, Alyssa, Ari, Benjamin, Bret, Erin, James, Justin, and Ryan

The Mad Scientist
©1996 Wright Group Publishing, Inc.
©1996 Story by Irene Schultz
Cover and cameo illustrations by Taylor Bruce
Interior illustrations by Meredith Yasui
Map illustration by Alicia Kramer

Woodland Mysteries™
©1996 Wright Group Publishing, Inc.

The Woodland Mysteries were created by the Wright Group development team.

The Wright Group
19201 120th Avenue NE
Bothell, WA 98011

Printed in the United States of America

10 9 8 7 6 5

ISBN: 0-7802-7229-3

What family solves mysteries...has adventures all over the world...and loves oatmeal cookies?

It's the Woodlanders!

Sammy Westburg (10 years old)
His sister Kathy Westburg (13)
His brother Bill Westburg (14)
His best friend Dave Briggs (16)
His best grown-up friend Mrs. Tandy
And Mop, their little dog!

The children all lost their parents, but with Mrs. Tandy have made their own family.

Why are they called the Woodlanders? Because they live in a big house in the Bluff Lake woods. On Woodland Street!

Together they find fun, mystery, and adventure. What are they up to now?

Read on!

Meet the Woodlanders!

Sammy Westburg
Sammy is a ten-year-old wonder! He's big for his fifth-grade class, and big-mouthed, too. He has wild hair and makes awful spider faces. Even so, you can't help liking him.

Bill Westburg
Bill, fourteen, is friendly and strong, and only one inch taller than his brother Sammy. He loves Sammy, but pokes him to make him be quiet! He's in junior high.

Kathy Westburg
Kathy, thirteen, is small, shy, and smart. She wants to be a doctor some day! She loves to be with Dave, and her brothers kid her about it. She's in junior high, too.

Dave Briggs

Dave, sixteen, is tall and blond. He can't walk, so he uses a wheelchair and drives a special car. He likes coaching high-school sports, solving mysteries, and reading. And Kathy!

Mrs. Tandy

Sometimes the kids call her Mrs. T. She's Becky Tandy, their tall, thin, caring friend. She's always ready for a new adventure, and for making cookies!

Mop

Mop is the family's little tan dog. Sometimes they have to leave him behind with friends. But he'd much rather be running after Sammy.

Table of Contents

Chapter   **Page**

1   The Copper Coin 1

2   I'm Scared 9

3   Dr. Frank N. Stein 15

4   A Really Nice Giant 25

5   Skeletons and Cookies 35

6   Frank N. Stein's Monster 43

7   Surprise on the Beach 53

8   Animal, Vegetable, or Mineral? 63

9   Peter Sticks Around 75

10 The Search Goes On 85

11 Some Kind of Trouble! 95

12 Don't Go, Sammy! 103

13 Prisoners 115

Chapter 1:
The Copper Coin

Ten-year-old Sammy Westburg raced into
the house in the woods.

"Hey, everybody! Look what I found!"
He waved his fist in the air.

"Bill!" he shouted. "Come look!"

His brother Bill, fourteen, came running into the dining room.

The boys' thirteen-year-old sister Kathy ran after him.

Sammy slapped a beautiful copper coin onto the dining-room table.

He yelled, "Mrs. Tandy! Dave! Come and see!"

In a minute all five members of the Woodland family were looking at the coin.

Dave Briggs, sixteen, picked it up. He rolled his wheelchair into better light. He said, "Hey, where did you get this, Sammy? It's really old."

Mrs. Tandy took one look at Sammy. She said, "Sammy, honey, you're as red as a stoplight. You need some water."

She brought him a drink from the kitchen.

He drank it all in one gulp.

Then he said, "I got so excited when I found the coin, I ran all the way home from right near the beach!"

Kathy said, "And it's the hottest out it's been all summer!"

Sammy nodded. "I bet it's near a hundred degrees. I feel like a sweat hog.

"Well, anyway, what kind of coin is it, Dave?"

Dave said, "Well, I know it isn't from the United States. It doesn't have a single English word on it."

Sammy said, "And do you see the date?

"I couldn't believe it when I saw the eighteen on the left side of the back and the zero-zero on the right!

"It's from 1800. That's about two hundred years ago!"

Mrs. Tandy said, "My lands! Think of it! That coin was made only twenty-four years after the American Revolution in 1776!"

Sammy said, "Maybe one of our first PRESIDENTS touched this coin!"

Dave said, "Hmm ... it's a little hard to read, but one word is FRANC."

Bill broke in. "Franc? So maybe it's an old coin from France!"

Dave said, "There's a hole drilled through it. And it's got all these scratches on it. It's too messed up for a coin collection."

Sammy said, "I don't care. It's the oldest thing I ever owned ... except for fossils. It's perfect for MY collection."

Dave kept reading from the coin. "Let's see, another word is REX."

Bill said, "That means king. And there's a picture of a man on it."

Kathy was starting to look worried. She asked, "Just where did you find this coin, Sammy?"

Sammy said, "That's the funny thing. It was on the sidewalk, on the corner across from the beach. You know, near that rusty old mail box."

Bill said, "I know where you mean. Near that thick forest. There's a house way back in there. You can hardly see it from the sidewalk."

Sammy said, "Yep, that's the corner. But wait a minute.

"I forgot to show you what else I found ... at the beach ... older than the coin ... millions of years older. I found some great fossil stones!"

He fished around in the pocket of his shorts. "Now where are they?"

He began to empty his pockets.

Bill grabbed a newspaper from a pile near the front door.

He put it on the table and said, "Here, un-load your pockets onto this."

Sammy laid out his things ...

a pocket knife

a ball of string

two packages of bubble gum

a pack of baseball cards

a blue rubber ball

a ball-point pen

a hard-boiled egg with the shell,
    cracked all over

... and one sock. (He was wearing only one with his shoes.)

Sammy said, "So HERE'S my other sock! I thought I lost it.

"Lucky we don't live any farther from the beach. My pockets were so heavy, my pants were about to fall down."

He came to the stones at last.

He brought out a sandy handful from the bottom of each pocket.

He said, "Look at them, but don't scratch them."

Bill said, "Don't scratch them!

"The ocean tossed these stones around for millions of years.

"Then they bumped around in our lake.

"Then animals walked on them on the beach, and sand blew against them.

"And you tell US not to scratch them?"

Sammy just stuck out his tongue.

Bill looked at the pile of fossils on the table. He said, "Well, Sammy. These are great. And so's the coin.

"But you might have to give it up."

Suddenly Sammy made his bull-dog face.

He said, "What do you mean, give it up?"

Chapter 2: I'm Scared

Bill said, "You have to go back to that old house in the woods.

"You have to at least ask the owner if that coin is his."

Dave said, "Right. I know how bad I'd feel if I had a coin like that and lost it."

Kathy said, "What if it was handed down in your family?

"What if your father gave it to you ... and you lost it?

"Maybe you'd better go right now, Sammy."

Sammy said, "Well ... maybe sometime. But not now. Too hot."

Bill said, "The weather guy said it would cool down a little later today."

Sammy said, "Well, I can't go today even if it goes down to zero.

"I have to ... uh ... clean my room."

Mrs. Tandy laughed. "Goodness! Cleaning your room never worried you before now!

"Why not clean it tomorrow?"

Sammy said, "Well, I can't go today,

anyway. I think I hurt my heel on a stone at the beach. Bad."

Kathy always took care of anyone who got hurt. She said, "Oh, no! Let me have a look at it."

Sammy took off his shoes ... and his other sock. He looked at the bottom of one foot, then the other.

He said, "I forgot which foot I hurt. Come to think of it, my heel feels OK again.

"But I still can't go today. I've got to walk Mop. He's begging for a really long walk."

Their furry little dog Mop lay under the table. He stretched and wagged his tail when he heard his name.

11

Then he went back to sleep. He began to snore a little.

Dave said, "It doesn't sound to me like he's begging for a walk. But if he is, why not take him over to that house?"

Finally Sammy blurted out, "Well, OK! I'll tell you why not!

"Because I CAN'T go there!

"Because I don't WANT to, that's why!

"Because by the time it's cool enough out, the sun will be going down.

"And that house is in a deep, dark woods!

"All huge bushes ... and thorns as tough as nails ... and twisty tree branches reaching down to grab you.

"And worst of all, you know who lives there?

"A MAD SCIENTIST!

"The kids say he comes out at the

crack of dawn.

"He wanders down to the beach alone. When other people come down to the beach, guess what he does?

"He hurries right past them, up the bluff. Then he cuts into his woods and disappears!

"Even if the people say hello he doesn't talk to them.

"If it's HIS coin, I wish I'd never found the old thing. Because I'm SCARED to go into his woods alone.

"THAT'S why I'm not going!"

Bill said, "ALONE? You wouldn't be going alone! I'll go with you!"

Kathy said, "Me, too, Sammy!"

Mrs. Tandy said, "I'm going, too. I wouldn't let my best boyfriend go alone to visit a mad scientist."

She gave Sammy a little hug.

Dave said, "All of us will go, Sammy. You know we stick together through thick and thin. And I guess this is the thick!"

Sammy grinned with relief.

He said, "Well, I guess I could go today after all."

He bragged, "Anyway, I wasn't really scared. I was just kidding, to see if you'd be too scared to go with me.

"Now here's my plan. When it cools down, we all go find the mad scientist!"

14

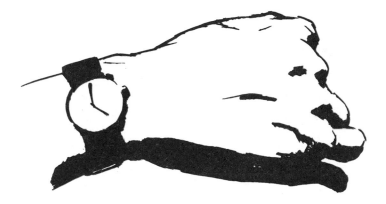

Chapter 3:
Dr. Frank N. Stein

Bill looked at his watch.

It was 5:00.

He said, "Well, I guess it's time to go."

Dave wheeled down the driveway.

The rest of the Woodlanders lagged after him.

Kathy had Mop on a leash. The little dog was wide awake now. He danced along at their side.

No one else was dancing.

No one had much to say.

They walked slowly for several blocks.

Then Mrs. Tandy said, "I guess we all feel a little afraid of this mad scientist. Maybe we should have asked Chief Hemster to go with us.

"Then we wouldn't be dragging our feet like this."

Sammy's mouth broke into a grin. He said, "No, you wouldn't be dragging your feet. You'd be dancing, because ..."

He darted a few feet away from her and sang, "Mrs. Tandy's got a b-o-o-o-y friend, Mrs. T. loves Chief Hem-m-ster."

Mrs. Tandy ran after him.

She called, "Catch him for me, everybody!"

They started chasing Sammy. Bill and Dave cornered him.

Then Kathy and Bill turned and chased Mrs. Tandy. After that they felt a lot more cheerful.

Finally they came to the bluff across from the beach. They looked into the thick woods.

They were thinking it didn't look too scary ... until Sammy said, in a creepy voice, "Here's where the mad scientist hides out."

Then he pointed to the sidewalk.
He said, "And that's where the coin was!"

Bill said, "Well, here we go, into the woods. I'll lead the way.

"The stone path is all bumpy. You push Dave's chair when it gets too bad, Sammy, and I'll pull."

17

They began to bump their way along the path.

It twisted from side to side into the deep, thick woods. The trees hid the sun from sight.

But even in the shade, the air felt hot. Not a breath of wind stirred the leaves.

They had to push hard on Dave's chair to make it move.

Every time they hit a bump, Sammy groaned, "Oops, sorry, Dave" or "Rats!" or "Gee, didn't see that one!"

Thorn bushes tore at their clothes and scratched their skin.

Finally Sammy said, "This guy must be a real weirdo! I bet he keeps the path like this so no one will come to see him!"

Dave said, "Well, if he's at home, he must know we are coming. Between Sammy groaning and my chair banging, we sound like an army moving in."

Mrs. Tandy said, "Look, there's the house. Why ... why ... it's a darling place, red with all that white trim.

"And the roof's wavy, like a gingerbread house in a fairy tale."

Bill said, "It doesn't look to me like anyone who's mean lives here. Look, there's even a hummingbird feeder."

He pointed to a tree branch next to the house. A tube of red sugar water hung from it.

Kathy said, "And look over to the right, Sammy. Isn't that a purple martin house on that pole?"

Sammy said, "OK, OK, I get the point. Someone who likes birds probably isn't all bad. So let's go meet him."

He ran up the front steps. He pressed the doorbell. He listened.

He didn't hear footsteps.

He said, "That's funny. There's a light on inside. It sure looks like someone's home."

He pressed the doorbell again, longer, three loud blasts. They could hear it ringing inside.

They listened for footsteps. They heard ... nothing.

Sammy banged on the door with his fists.

Nothing.

He turned around and said, "After all that work getting here, no one's home. We tried. Now can I keep the coin?"

Bill said, "Good try, Sammy, but no. We will just have to try again tomorrow."

Dave said, "Before we leave, let's take a look in back. Maybe someone's working there and doesn't hear us."

They went around to the back of the house.

They saw ...

a birdbath

a sundial

a stone bench

a Chinese garden seat

a wind sock

21

a garden full of vegetables and flowers
... and roses growing over an archway.

Kathy said softly, "Well, even if there's
no one home I'm glad we came. It's so
pretty back here."

Sammy said, "Well, I guess it won't be
so bad, coming back tomorrow."

They went around to the front again.

Mrs. Tandy said, "Just one more try."

She walked up the steps and gave the doorbell a long ring. Then she leaned closer to read a little brass sign above the bell.

She said, "Well, at least we know who lives here. It says Dr. Frank N. Stein."

Sammy gave a loud yip. Then he cried, "DR. FRANKENSTEIN? Get me out of here!"

Mrs. Tandy laughed. "Not Dr. Frankenstein, the one who made a monster. It's Dr. Frank-N.-Stein.

"But no one's answering the doorbell, anyway, so why don't we head for the library?"

But at that very minute, BANG! THE DOOR FLEW OPEN!

Chapter 4:
A Really Nice Giant

A flood of light poured out the open door.

In the middle of the light stood a BIG MAN ... a HUGE man.

But with the light shining through it, his hair glowed like a cloud of white fire.

His loud voice boomed out, "WHO'S THERE?"

Mop barked and began running in circles. His leash wound around Sammy's legs.

Bill grabbed a thick branch from the ground. He held it up, ready to protect everyone.

They were all so scared they were shaking.

The man shouted, "COME UP HERE SO I CAN SEE YOU BETTER. AND TALK SLOWLY!"

By then Sammy had hold of Bill's other arm, tight, like a pair of pliers.

Bill whispered out of the side of his mouth, "Let's get out of here."

Dave whispered, "Everybody start backing away slowly."

Then the man shouted, "TELL ME IF I'M TALKING TOO LOUD. I'M DEAF. I CAN'T HEAR YOU. I CAN'T EVEN HEAR MYSELF.

"I HOPE I DIDN'T KEEP YOU WAITING LONG.

"I WAS IN MY LAB WITH MY BACK TO THE DOORBELL LIGHT.

"THEN I HAPPENED TO TURN AROUND AND SEE IT BLINKING.

"I DROPPED MY GLASSES IN MY HURRY TO GET HERE. AND I'M NEAR-SIGHTED. VERY NEAR-SIGHTED. YOU'LL HAVE TO COME UP CLOSER SO I CAN READ YOUR LIPS."

He stepped back into the house.

Now the light fell on his face.

Mrs. Tandy whispered, "Why, he doesn't look like a mad scientist to me! He looks nice!"

Kathy said, "And he can't tell how loud

27

he's talking. THAT'S why he's yelling!"

Everyone let out a sigh of relief.

They all helped Dave up the steps.

Dave said, "Can you read my lips now? Are we close enough?"

"THAT'S FINE!" he shouted. Then he saw them move back again.

"Oh," he said more quietly. "How's this? I haven't talked to anyone for several weeks.

"I'm Frank Stein. What can I do for you?"

His wild white hair didn't look scary now. It looked soft and shining. And his big face was full of wrinkles and smiles.

Sammy walked right up to him.

He said, "You're big! Like a giant!"

Then he was afraid he had insulted Dr. Stein. So he added, "I mean a really nice giant."

The doctor laughed. "All right, all right. So I'm a nice giant. And who are you people?"

Dave said, "Well, I'm Dave. This is Sammy and Kathy and Mrs. Tandy and Bill."

Mrs. Tandy broke in. "But you can just call me Becky."

Dave went on. "And Sammy has something to show you."

Sammy said, "I found this today near your mailbox.

"We thought it might be yours."

Dr. Stein took the coin. He held it up for a good look.

Then he smiled and nodded.

His face broke into a grin.

He said, "I'm so glad to get this back. I felt terrible when I couldn't find it. Thank you so much.

"I always meant to discover where it came from, but never took the time. I've had it for seventy years, ever since I was ten years old."

Sammy said, "Hey! That's exactly how old I am now!

"So ... how did your coin get outside?"

Dr. Stein said, "I always keep it in my lab ... on a table where I sometimes work.

"When I got up to get the mail today I must have knocked the coin off.

"I guess somehow it stuck in my clothes.

"Then it must have fallen off when I

leaned over to get my mail."

Sammy said, "It's a wonderful coin. Maybe someday I'll find out for you what country it came from."

Bill said, "Well, we have to run along. It was nice meeting you."

Dr. Stein didn't answer.

Then Bill realized the doctor hadn't heard him. So he touched Dr. Stein's arm. Then he said good-bye again.

Dr. Stein said, "No, no, no. You must not go without a little visit and some iced tea. And cookies and honey cake. I baked them myself!

"I love to bake. Baking is like doing chemistry.

"You mix up a mess of runny stuff.

"You heat it up.

"It comes out solid, filled with tiny bubbles and good tastes.

"How did it turn from runny stuff into solid cake? It's a mystery of chemistry.

"And maybe now you'd like to look around.

"Come in, come right in."

Dave said, "I'd love to ... if it's all right with everybody else."

Mrs. Tandy said, "We'd all love a cold glass of tea."

They followed Dr. Stein inside.

Sammy took one look around. He

said, "Holy bananas!"

There was a room as big as a whole one-story house!

That room was filled with glass-covered cases ...

old wooden tools

a telescope

microscopes

a big TV screen

a stove

a giant double sink

test tubes and chemical mixes

... and dried plants hanging upside-down in bunches from the ceiling.

But mostly, there were shelves lining all the walls.

And tables everywhere, covered with the strangest things the Woodlanders had ever seen.

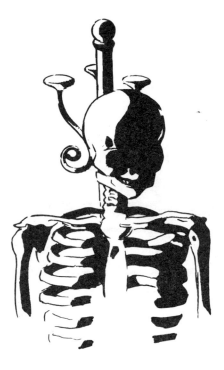

Chapter 5:
Skeletons and Cookies

They stood and stared.
    They saw ...
    stuffed birds
    pots of young plants

drawing pencils
paints
papers

old books
new books
deer horns
brass horns
a stuffed fish
drawings
bird nests
bird eggs
cocoons

a stuffed ferret
a life-sized plastic human body
skulls and long bones
colorful rocks
bags and boxes of cooking stuff
canned foods
garden tools
wasp nests
fossil rocks
... and butterflies and moths.

And hanging from a hat stand in one corner was a human skeleton.

Sammy screamed, and pointed at the skeleton. He said, "Look at THAT!

"Are you really a mad scientist, like the kids say? Does the police chief know about that skeleton?"

Dr. Stein laughed. "So you know John Hemster, too? He drops in quite often for tea and a visit.

"I'm certainly not a mad scientist! Not either kind of mad! Not crazy-mad ... or angry-mad!"

Sammy said, "Well, the chief's our best friend. So I guess if you're his friend, you're OK with us."

The others had been wandering around, mouths open.

Mrs. Tandy said, "My lands! This is some house, Dr. Stein!"

Kathy said, "It's not just a house. It's a museum!"

Dave wheeled around the room, looking.

His eyes shone with excitement.

At last he stopped in front of Dr. Stein. He said, "I love your place. It's just wonderful!"

Dr. Stein looked pleased.

He said, "Well, let's have some of that tea!"

He got a big, icy pitcher from the refrigerator.

He handed around a plate of chocolate butter cookies and honey spice cake with raisins in it.

Kathy said thank you, but he didn't hear her. So she waved her hand a little to get his attention. Then she said thank you while he was watching her.

After that, that's how they all talked to him.

Sammy waved and asked, "So, are you really a doctor?"

Dr. Stein said, "No, a scientist. The doctor in my name is because I spent many years studying science in college."

Sammy munched a cookie and said, "What do you do here all day? Are you here alone all the time? Don't you get pretty lonely?"

Dr. Stein said, "Most of the time I'm alone, but I'm all right. I'm always doing something interesting."

Mrs. Tandy took a piece of cake and asked, "Do you have any visitors besides Chief Hemster?"

The doctor said, "Once in a while my sister's grandson, my grandnephew Peter, comes by. To tell you the truth, I don't think he comes to keep me company.

"The boy is always short on money. He counts on me to give him a little before he leaves.

"Now he's dropped out of school. Says he needs time to find himself ... I don't know what that means.

"He's eighteen, and he doesn't work. My sister, poor thing, ends up paying his way!"

The doctor sounded sad.

To change the subject, Bill said, "Hey, I see you collect fossils! We do, too!

"Sammy even found some today!

"So how come we never run into you ... collecting down on the beach?"

The big man gave a little smile and said, "I walk down the bluff very early, around five-thirty in the morning.

"I plan my walk so I won't meet anybody. You see, if I'm not looking up, I can't tell when people are talking to me.

"And after all, I can't ask everyone to stand right in front of me to talk.

"It would be a lot of trouble for them. So I stick to myself pretty much."

Now Sammy was munching down another cookie.

With his mouth full he blurted out, "I think you're wrong. People would love to talk to you. You are VERY wrong!"

And with that, a bunch of cookie crumbs shot out of his mouth ... and landed all over Dr. Stein's shirt.

Chapter 6:
Frank N. Stein's Monster

Dr. Stein stared down at his crumb-covered shirt.

All Mrs. Tandy could think of to say was, "OOPS!"

Bill and Dave just sat with their mouths open.

Kathy felt her cheeks burning red.

But good old Sammy stayed calm.

He reached straight out to Dr. Stein's stomach.

He brushed off the cookie crumbs fast, one-two-three.

He kept right on talking. "So why don't you wear a hearing aid, like my friend Kenny at school does?

"He could barely hear at all. But now he has a hearing aid, and he lip reads, too.

"And don't anybody poke me for asking. I bet you're all wondering the same thing."

Dr. Stein laughed, LOUD.

He put his arm around Sammy's shoulders.

He said, "So they poke you when you

say what's on your mind? Well, I will protect you."

Sammy stuck his tongue out at Bill.

Dr. Stein said, "It's good to ask questions. That's one way to get answers.

"I tried hearing aids fifteen years ago. They buzzed in my ear. Too much trouble. Besides, I get along fine without them."

Sammy said, "Hey, that's just what Kenny says about computers!

"He won't use a computer unless he has to in class. Says they're too much trouble. Says he can get along fine without them."

Dr. Stein said, "My, I could never get along without my computer!"

Sammy blabbed right on, "That's what Kenny says about his hearing aid!

"Well, pass the cookies, please. You're a really great cookie chemist, Dr. Stein!"

This time Sammy took TWO cookies. He walked over to a shelf.

He stopped in front of a huge, bag-shaped gray thing … about as big as he was. He touched it.

He said, "What's this? It feels like it's made of dry old paper."

Dr. Stein said, "Well, my little friend with the big questions, it IS paper. Paper made by wasps. You're touching the big-gest wasp nest on record."

"A WASP nest!" Sammy traveled backward five feet in one jump! "WASPS! ICK! Is one on me, Bill?"

Dr. Stein said, "No need to worry. Those wasps all died out long ago. Go ahead, you can touch the nest.

"All of you, you can touch anything in the house.

"The only place off-limits is my lab.

"See the two doors down at the end of the house? The one on the right leads to my bedroom and bath.

"The other one, with the lock hanging on it, is my lab. I allow no one in it unless I'm there.

"Now go look around!"

The Woodlanders began to stare at everything.

Dave pointed to the life-sized model of a human body.

He said, "We had one of those plastic

47

models in biology class. But our liver got ruined in a chemical spill.

"Our teacher had to borrow a plastic liver for us to study."

Dr. Stein said, "Why, I am the friend she borrowed the extra liver from! You were studying MY liver ... well, my plastic man's liver.

"I hardly ever use it anymore. I told your teacher to keep it until I needed it. It's still over at the high school."

Bill pointed to a huge, worn-looking book.

He said, "What's that, Dr. Stein?"

Dr. Stein said, "That's my favorite book. It's a dictionary of every word in the English language. It even tells where each word comes from.

"If I had to choose only one book to read for the rest of my life, that's the one I'd pick."

Kathy said, "You study words, too?"

Dr. Stein said, "I wish I could study everything, the world's so full of interesting things.

"As it is, I study atoms and the energy that comes from them.

"And I study living animals and fossils.

"I study wild plants used for food or medicine.

"And I study the ways different people live."

Bill laughed. "Anything else?"

Dr. Stein said, "Well, I study how the human body works."

Kathy said, "That's part of what I want to do. I want to be a doctor ... Dr. Westburg!"

Dr. Stein smiled. "That's wonderful, Kathy! We will both be doctors!"

Mrs. Tandy said, "What else do you do? Do you have other scientist friends?"

The doctor nodded. "I talk with other scientists at the Science Club of America. They publish my writings in their magazine."

Sammy said, "How can you talk with

them if you can't hear them?"

Dr. Stein said, "Our computers are linked by modems! A modem hooks into your computer like a phone line.

"I send my papers on the computer, and we talk by typing.

"And if I have a question, I simply type it in. My modem lets me put it out on a computer bulletin board. I get answers right away!"

Sammy said, "Kenny should hear this. Maybe then he'd give computers a chance."

Bill looked at his watch and said, "Hey, we better be going. You're probably busy ... and we want to go to the library today, too."

Dr. Stein said, "This visit was so pleasant. I hope you'll come again soon!"

Sammy said, "You bet! You know, you're not bad for a mad scientist."

51

This time Bill DID poke him. He said, "Stop calling him that, Sammy. Don't be a monster."

Sammy said, "Stop poking me, Mr. Perfect.

"Dr. Stein, some people think you're a mad scientist, but I like you.

"And you like me even if I am a monster. So I'll be YOUR monster!

"Dr. Frank N. Stein's monster! That's me!

"And I am coming back. And I'm bringing a friend, OK?"

At that, EVERYONE poked him.

But Dr. Stein said, "Don't hurt my monster. Monsters have rights, too. So please do bring your friend, Sammy."

Sammy said, "I will. And sooner than you think."

Chapter 7:
Surprise on the Beach

It was still dark at 4:45 the next morning.

RAT-A-TAT-TAT-TAT-TAT!

Sammy woke up with a start.

RAT-A-TAT-TAT-TAT-TAT!

It sounded like a small jackhammer outside his window.

Sammy frowned. It was the mixed-up woodpecker again, pecking on the drainpipe.

RAT-A-TAT ...

Sammy tapped on the windowpane.

Mop ran into the room, barking at all the noise.

The woodpecker flew away screaming, "Hyak, hyak, hyak."

Sammy said, "That little rat! First he wakes me up. Then he laughs at me.

"Well, I was going to get up early anyway. Time to get going on my plan!"

He turned off his alarm clock.

He raced out to the bathroom in his underwear. Mop raced after him.

Sammy ran a little water into a cup.

Then he padded barefoot to the other end of the house.

He sneaked into Bill and Dave's room. He stood between their beds.

He dipped his fingers into the cup.

He shook his dripping wet hand over their faces and turned to run away.

Bill jumped out of bed like a kangaroo.

He shouted, "Yikes! It's Frank N. Stein's monster!"

He grabbed his pillow and threw it at Sammy.

Sammy spun around and leaped backward. Dave threw his pillow and got Sammy in the stomach.

Sammy said, "Hey, stop it! You guys are lucky it was just a little water that woke you up.

"What if you woke up like I did ... with a tin drum outside your window!"

Bill said, "Oh, so the crazy woodpecker was at it again? Well, it's looking for a really big bug. That's why it chooses your room."

Sammy sang out, "Sticks and stones will break my bones, but names will never hurt me."

Then he added, "Get dressed, you guys. I've got a great plan.

"I called my friend last night.

"It's time for him to meet the mad scientist! Right now! At the beach!"

Bill said, "Wait a minute, Sammy.

What if Dr. Stein gets mad? What if he doesn't want to meet anybody while he's fossil hunting?"

Without answering, Sammy ran out of their room, and over to his bedroom.

He grabbed some clothes and a kazoo. He ran to Kathy's room.

He hummed into his kazoo, loud.

Kathy threw open her door. "What's happening?"

She rubbed her eyes and opened them wide, but she didn't look awake.

Mrs. Tandy came running from her room. "Good heavens, Sammy! What's all the noise about?

"Between the woodpecker and your kazoo, it sounds like a marching band is passing our house!"

Sammy said, "Well, I had to wake everyone up for my surprise!"

He said, "We are taking a breakfast

picnic down to the beach!"

Mrs. Tandy said, "What fun!"

Sammy said, "I knew you'd like it. So you're in charge of hot dogs and buns. For seven people!

"And Kathy, you pack the pop!"

He grabbed some shorts and a T-shirt out of his room. He hopped around, pulling them on. Then he darted all the way back to Bill and Dave's room.

He said, "You guys, we are going to make breakfast at the beach. You pack some marshmallows and potatoes to roast.

"We can find driftwood there to make a fire.

"I'll get paper plates and napkins and cups and matches.

"Let's get a move on! My friend will be at the beach around five-thirty!" Then Sammy ran into the kitchen.

When everybody was ready to go,

they piled the stuff into Dave's special car. He could work the brakes and gas from handles near the steering wheel.

Dave drove down the bluff road to unload.

They carried him in his chair across the sand to their favorite picnic spot.

Mrs. Tandy drove the car back up the bluff to park it.

She was starting to walk back down when a big voice called, "Why, it's Becky Tandy! What a nice surprise!"

Dr. Stein was heading out of the woods.

Mrs. Tandy called, "Why, Frank Stein! Hello!" The two walked on together.

Then they noticed a boy walking down to the beach in front of them.

Mrs. Tandy shouted, "Kenny! Kenny Abdul! Hi, there!"

The boy turned around.

He grinned and waved. He waited for them to catch up.

He said, "Hi, Mrs. Tandy! Sammy invited me to meet him here."

Mrs. Tandy said, "Dr. Stein, this is Sammy's friend Kenny Abdul."

Kenny said, "Hello. Where's Sammy? Oh, there he is!"

He saw them all below, putting potatoes on the fire.

Mop, all wet, was rolling in the sand ... and shaking it all over everyone.

Mrs. Tandy, Dr. Stein, and Kenny went on down.

Sammy had a stick with two bubbly brown marshmallows on it.

He held them toward Dr. Stein.

He said all in one breath, "Here, try these ... they're the start of our surprise picnic breakfast for you!

"The potatoes will be ready in half an hour ... you can hunt fossils till then ... Bill said you might be mad ... you're not mad at us, are you?"

Dr. Stein said, "So you think I might be mad, do you?"

He stretched his long arms up in the air above Sammy to grab him.

His big fingers curled like claws.

To Sammy, Dr. Stein looked sort of like Frankenstein's monster himself!

Chapter 8: Animal, Vegetable, or Mineral?

Dr. Stein grabbed Sammy ... and hugged him!

He was grinning.

He said, "Of course I'm not mad! I

told you I almost never get mad.

"And why should I get mad at you?

"I LOVE surprises, my dear monster. Now, let's hunt fossils."

Dr. Stein sat down on a big patch of gravel. He began looking at stones.

The others carried Dave over to a towel on the gravel.

In a second Bill said, "Hey! I found a crinoid cup!" He said the word like this: CRY-noid.

Dave said, "That's great, Bill! We've found tons of crinoid stems. You know, like what Sammy found. But no crinoid CUP.

"I've only seen them in museums!"

Kenny said, "Hey, this is cool! Maybe I'll start collecting fossils."

Kathy took the small stone and turned it over.

She said, "It looks a little like a tiny stone heart."

Dave said, "It's weird to think it used to be part of a live animal.

"A whole crinoid looks like a flower.

"Some people call them sea lilies."

Sammy said, "All right, all right. I bet you've read a million books about crinoids, right?"

Mean while, Kathy had found a brain-coral fossil, and Mrs. Tandy found a clear print of a lamp shell in a stone.

Soon Bill said, "I bet the potatoes are ready! Let's go eat!"

They carried Dave back to his chair.

■ ■ ■

They didn't know someone was watching their every move.

Up on the bluff a young man stared down through the trees.

After a moment he darted into the doctor's woods.

■ ■ ■

Bill was saying, "Here are roasting sticks for the hot dogs. When you've cooked yours, I'll put them onto buns for you."

Sammy got his hot dog all ready to eat. Then he found a spider crawling on it. While Bill was brushing the spider off, he ate Bill's hot dog.

Yelling like Tarzan, Bill chased him

into the water.

Sammy splashed Bill and chased him back out. Then they came back for more hot dogs.

Soon some other people walked down from the bluff.

Dr. Stein said, "This has been very fine ... but I would like to get home now. Do come back with me."

So they soaked the fire with water.

They cleaned up their mess.

Mrs. Tandy got the car and picked Dave up from the beach.

Then they pushed their way along Dr. Stein's path.

He said, "I like to keep my woods wild, but it's too over-grown now.

"Bushes growing onto the path ... buckthorn trees taking over ... dead branches everywhere. Just look around.

"I tried to hire my grandnephew

Peter to prune it, but he says he's too busy."

Kathy said, "Hey, we are looking for summer jobs. We can do it for you!"

Kenny said, "I need a job, too!"

Dr. Stein said, "Wonderful! When could you all start?"

Dave said, "What's wrong with today? Right now?"

Dr. Stein clapped his hands. He said, "Perfect! And before we go inside, I'll tell you about another job. Do you like mysteries?"

Bill said, "Do we like mysteries? Do we like mysteries? Do fleas like dogs? We LOVE mysteries!"

Dr. Stein said, "Well, you know the coin Sammy returned to me? Believe it or not, I have three bags of very old coins. They were my family's.

"They're gold or silver ... and they don't have holes in them, either.

"They're worth a great deal of money.

"I should have kept them at the bank, but I liked looking at them.

"Now I've decided to sell them. I want to start a fund to send young people to college to study science.

"But I've put those coins away somewhere, and I can't remember where!"

Mrs. Tandy laughed, and said, "I know the feeling!"

Kathy said, "What did the bags look like?"

69

Dr. Stein said, "They were just about the size of a fist. Not my fist." His was huge. "Maybe Becky's fist."

He went on. "Well, I know how I lost them. For years I kept my things just anywhere. I remembered where everything was. But one day I decided to be NEAT.

"I decided to store everything in groups ... animal, vegetable, or mineral."

Kathy said, "What did you do with the mixed things, like that stuffed bird on a branch?"

Dr. Stein said, "I put those into another group ... mixtures.

"Now I'm in a real MESS! I don't know where half my things are. And I can't find my coins.

"I searched for them in the MINERAL group because they're metal.

"Then I looked in the ANIMAL area

because there are pictures of people on most of them, and people are animals.

"Then I searched the VEGETABLE area because the coin bags are made of cotton cloth.

"And last week I searched through MIXTURES."

Sammy said, "Well, you can stop worrying. We can find your coins, no problem!"

Dr. Stein said, "I mentioned them to Peter a few weeks ago. He asked me a thousand questions about where I thought they might be.

"But then he said he was too busy to go on a wild goose chase."

Bill said, "Well, WE aren't too busy to look for them. It'll be fun!"

71

Sammy said, "We should put Dave in charge of planning the hunt. He's the best at planning. The rest of us can start trimming these woods."

Dr. Stein took out his key to let them into the house.

Just then Mop began barking.

A tall, well-dressed young man slipped around from the back of the house.

He walked toward them with both hands in his pockets.

He said in a sugary-sweet voice, "Hi, my good old Unc. I came to visit you." Then he said, "What are these strangers doing here?"

His eyes darted around at them.

Dr. Stein said, "These are my new friends, Peter."

Everyone said hello. Peter just looked at each one of them, up and down.

Dr. Stein said, "Dave, let's get you inside so you can start planning the coin search."

Peter said, "COIN search! Just a minute! Just a little minute, Unc!

"You're letting STRANGERS look for your coins! That's stupid!"

Dr. Stein said, "But, Peter, you told me you were way too busy to do it.

"Besides, these aren't strangers. I told you, these are my friends."

The doctor pushed open the front door.

But he stopped dead in his tracks.

He spoke so quietly, he almost whispered. "Someone comes into this house when I'm out. This time I'm sure."

Chapter 9:
Peter Sticks Around

Mrs. Tandy said, "How do you know someone's been inside?"

Dr. Stein said, "Well, I've had a funny feeling about it for weeks."

Peter said, "You're just getting old, Unc. You're imagining things."

Dr. Stein shook his head. "No. I'm not imagining this. The other day I found some of my books out of place.

"And the day before I saw some dried leaves inside the door.

"This morning I decided I'd find out for sure. So I closed the front door on a sheet of paper, right up here."

He pointed high up on the door frame.

"When I opened the door just now I didn't see it float down. The paper was already lying on the floor.

"See, there it is. Did you see it fall?"

Everyone said no. Everyone but Peter.

Peter said, "Sure, I saw it float down. It's just that your eyes aren't so sharp anymore."

Dr. Stein said, "Well, that may be.

But since you're here, my boy, maybe you'd like to help prune the woods."

Peter looked at the others. "Er, just when are you going to start the coin search?"

Dave said, "We could start it tomorrow. OK, guys?"

Peter said, "Well, I just remembered, I have to be somewhere. There's no way I can prune today. I'll come back to help tomorrow.

"Hey, Unc, I'm flat broke. Let me have a few bucks, will you? After all, my birthday's coming up soon."

Dr. Stein said, "Here's a little money. And good-bye, my boy."

Then Bill said, "Hey, Dave. I have another idea. YOU start the coin search TODAY. You and Kathy. Inside, where it's cool.

"It's going to be a scorcher, and you

don't do well in too much heat."

Mrs. Tandy said, "Good idea. I'll work with the others outside. I'm tall enough to cut the high branches. Well, nice meeting you, Peter. Good-bye!"

But Peter said, "Just a minute! You're starting the coin search today? I'm not leaving! I'm staying to help look for those coins."

Then he winked at Kathy and added, "Kathy wants me to stay, too."

Her face turned red. She took a step closer to Dave.

Dave said, "What about your important plans, Peter?"

Peter said, "I'll skip them. Anything to help out old Unc."

Dr. Stein said, "Fine. I thought you said it was a wild goose chase. I'm glad you changed your mind.

"Come along, my dear Becky. Since

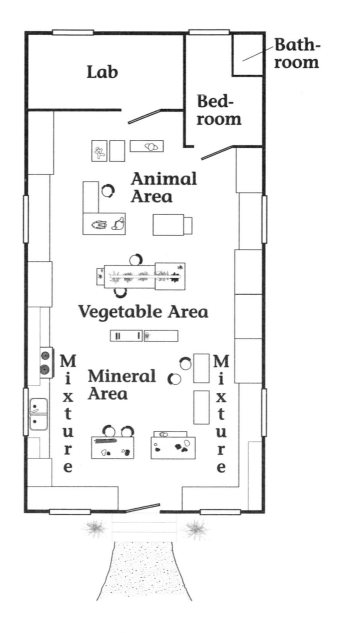

Lab

Bath-room

Bed-room

Animal Area

Vegetable Area

Mineral Area

Mixture

Mixture

you'll be outside, I think I will work outside myself today."

Sammy poked Bill and whispered, "Mrs. T. has a new B-O-Y-Y-Y friend."

Then he grinned and trotted outside.

Once inside Dave looked all around the huge room.

He said to Kathy, "Looks to me like the ANIMAL area is down at the end, near the lab. See those stuffed animals and the model of the human body?"

Kathy nodded. "And the VEGETABLE group is just this side of it. Look at all the dried plants hanging above the tables."

Dave said, "And next to that, the MINERALS. See the rocks on the tables? And pieces of different metals?

"And the MIXTURE group is all around us.

"The doctor has his fossils in this

group ... I guess because fossils start out as animals or vegetables, and end up as stones.

"We might as well start right here. The shelves first.

"Kathy, you do those middle ones.

"I can reach the lower ones and the floor from my chair.

"Peter, you do the highest shelves."

Peter said, "No way, man. You get to work yourself. I'm going to rest. Come sit down with me, Kathy."

He sagged down on a bench.

He pulled out a pack of cigarettes and lit one.

He blew a cloud of smoke right in Dave's face.

Kathy wrinkled her nose.

She waved the smoke away from Dave.

Dave said, "Come on, Kathy. Let's

you and I start. We can ask Mrs. Tandy
to help with the high shelves later."

They hunted quietly for a while.

Then Kathy said, "Here are some white
plastic bags. They feel like they're full of
small stones."

Dave said, "Maybe the coins are in there! I guess we have to empty them, Kathy. Dr. Stein might have taken the coins out of their cotton bags."

Peter said, "Hah! You poor saps. You're going to be working forever. You couldn't get through this mountain of boring junk in a year."

Dave said, "Boring junk! It's the most interesting stuff I've ever seen!"

Kathy said, "And we will get through it just fine, without your help!"

Peter said, "OK, you dorks. Work all you want.

"I'm sitting right here keeping an eye on you.

"And don't get any ideas about stealing those coins!

"I'm Dr. Stein's grandnephew.

"Those coins belong to ME!

"You find them, you hand them over to ME!"

Chapter 10:
The Search Goes On

Slowly Dave wheeled over to Peter.

He said, "Wait a minute, Peter. Let's get this straight.

"Dr. Stein asked us to try to find his coins.

"I wouldn't even THINK of keeping them.

"And I would never turn them over to you, either. They're his.

"So lie around and watch us if you want, but keep your big mouth shut."

Peter sneered, "Oh, right, boss.

"You're going to make me? From your wheelchair? Don't make me laugh."

Dave's strong arms ached to punch Peter's sneering face.

Just then there was a noise at the door.

Quick as a cat, Peter stamped his cigarette flat on the wooden floor.

He kicked it under a table.

Dr. Stein came inside. The rest followed after him.

The doctor said, "This air-conditioning feels so good. It's really too hot to work outside. I'm going to mix a little iced tea for us."

He pointed to four huge cans on a shelf near the sink.   He grinned at Mrs. Tandy and asked, "Think I have enough tea?"

Kathy said, "That's enough tea to last for ten years in a restaurant!"

Dr. Stein said, "I bought them from a restaurant supply house.

"I figured the tea would be easy to make. It has sugar mixed right in!

"But somehow I thought the cans

would get used up faster ... "

Sammy said, "You may be drinking that tea for the rest of your life!"

Bill poked Sammy in the ribs.

Sammy poked back.

Kenny laughed.

Then they all sat down to drink the tea.

Dr. Stein sniffed and said, "Peter, you know I've asked you not to smoke in here. I hate the smell.

"And what's worse, that dirty smoke can give you lung cancer."

Peter stood up and said, "There you go imagining things again, Unc. I wasn't smoking. Do you see a cigarette?"

He held up his hands and turned them front and back.

Then he said, "You're really losing it, Unc, blaming me. Maybe Dave, here, was sneaking a smoke. I wouldn't know.

I was busy looking for your coins."

Quietly Dave said, "I don't smoke." But his eyes were flashing mad.

Peter went on. "Anyway, talk about dirt! This whole house is full of it!

"A hundred years of dirt and germs, lying around your old junk.

"Dirty old rocks ... and jars of dirt ... and germy snake skins ... and rusty old tools ... and dirty bones ...

"And these kids, they'll never find your coins. They're only goofing off ... messing things up more.

"And who knows what they would do with the coins if they did find them. Probably keep them."

Dr. Stein started to answer, but Bill had already jumped to his feet.

He was only about Sammy's size, but he was boiling mad. He looked BIG.

Peter fell back onto the bench.

Bill said, "Listen, Peter, my back is to Dr. Stein. He can't tell what I'm saying. I'm calling you a DIRTY LIAR!

"First you better tell him you take back what you just said ... about his house and about Kathy and Dave.

"And then you'd better watch your big mouth. And if you don't, you're going to have to deal with ME."

Peter saw the look on Bill's face. He got scared.

He walked over to Dr. Stein. He said, "Unc, I was only joking. These kids are all right.

"And believe me, your house is great, really great. I love it.

"In fact, I'm coming every day. I'll work right along with the others.

"Just tell me what to do next, Dave. You're the boss." And he pretended to be listening for orders.

Dave decided everyone should search in the MIXTURE group.

In a minute Dr. Stein called out, "Look! Right in this drawer!

"My monkey carved from a peach pit! My favorite aunt gave me this, and I was afraid it was lost forever!

"I remember! I couldn't decide if I should store it in ANIMAL or VEGETABLE. So I put it in MIXTURE!"

Sammy said, "Listen, Dr. Stein. I think you should store things your old way ... the way I do in my room.

"Just put things anyplace where you can SEE them. It's a little messy, but you'll find them when you need to."

Dr. Stein smiled. He said, "That's what I'm going to do from now on."

At noon Dave said, "We really have to stop now. Kenny and Sammy have a ball game at two.

"And we have to get stuff ready for the neighborhood picnic dinner. And the croquet games are tonight." He said the word like this: crow-KAY.

Sammy said, "But we can come back tomorrow."

Dr. Stein said, "I'll look for you then.

I'm glad you brought Kenny. I wish you two weren't busy tonight.

"I'm sending a paper on my computer modem. I wanted to show you how it works. I bet you would love it, Kenny. Well, I'll see you all tomorrow!"

Outside Peter waited until Mrs. Tandy walked past, out of earshot.

He turned to the others and said, "Don't come near Uncle Frank before tomorrow, understand? I don't want him bothered by a bunch of strangers."

Bill just laughed.

Sammy said, "Go sit on a tack, Peter."

Peter gave them a long, mean look.

Then he darted off into the woods.

Chapter 11:
Some Kind of Trouble!

Kathy kept shaking her head.

She said, "Peter really scares me."

Kenny said, "If you ask me, that kid is bad news."

Dave looked grim. He said, "I feel sorry for Dr. Stein. Imagine having to be nice to Peter because he's your grand-nephew."

Sammy said, "Not so grand, if you ask me."

Mrs. Tandy said, "For a minute there, Bill, I thought you were going to punch him. I know it was hard not to.

"He's got a mouth on him like the Grand Canyon."

Kathy said, "I even thought Dave was going to give him one in the jaw."

By now Sammy was jumping around. He hit the air and shouted, "GOTCHA, Peter! Take that, you rat! POW! And that! BOOM! POW! GOTCHA!"

He almost hit Bill.

Bill grabbed Sammy's wrists and said, "All right, prize fighter. Save it for your ball game."

Kenny walked home, and the Woodlanders went to make lunch.

After eating, Sammy packed up food for the picnic dinner that night.

He packed turkey slices ... and bread ... and mustard ... and tomatoes ... and apples ... and orange juice.

Mrs. Tandy added a big bowl of potato salad.

She said, "This is for the potluck table."

Bill said, "Mrs. T., that's HUGE!"

Sammy said, "No, it's not just huge,

it's eNORmous!"

Kathy said, "It's not just enormous, it's giGANtic!"

Dave said, "It's not just gigantic, it's imMENSE!"

Mrs. Tandy laughed. "Well, maybe I did over-do it a little. I wanted everyone at the picnic to have a taste. I sure hope they like it."

Sammy said, "I sure hope they don't! I love your potato salad. I'll eat it all if no one else does."

Dave said, "Well, let's go, everyone! Are we taking Mop?"

Sammy said, "Of course! You guys watch him during the ball game. Kenny and I will keep track of him after.

"I know he won't be any trouble during the croquet game. Last time he stopped a croquet ball with his nose.

"Now he runs away when a croquet

ball comes near him!"

They loaded the car and headed for the park.

The baseball game was over by 5:00. It was a tie.

Sammy said, "We should have won. I still think I was safe that time at third. The ump needs new glasses!"

Dave said, "I was the ump, and I never wear glasses."

Bill said, "Thank goodness it was a tie, or we would never hear the end of this. And it's too hot to argue."

THE MAD SCIENTIST

All the families un-packed their sandwiches and potluck dishes.

Plop! A wet drop hit Bill's nose.

He said, "Did you feel anything,
guys?"

A few drops hit the others.

Then all in a rush the rain came.

It didn't just shower. It poured. It
pounded. It flowed. It flooded.

People ran in all directions in the
warm downpour.

Soaking wet, the Woodlanders raced to
their car.

Bill said, "OK, Dave, start it up. But
wait, where's Sammy?"

Suddenly Sammy came running up.

He said, "I just helped Kenny's family
load their car. What a mix-up! Half the
sandwiches aren't even theirs!

"They invited me to have dinner with
them. Can I? I'll come back home by

100

nine. And I'll take Mop with me for protection."

Mrs. Tandy laughed. "Some protection ... about what you'd get from a mouse. But I don't see why not. Have fun!"

It was 9:00 and Sammy wasn't home yet.

At 9:30 Bill called Kenny's house.

Kenny's mother said, "I'm worried, too. Three hours ago the boys took Mop to play in the rain. They said they would be back here by eight-fifteen."

Bill said, "Did they say anything about going someplace?"

Mrs. Abdul said, "Not one word."

Just then Kathy heard a scratching sound at the front door. Then a bark.

She said, "I hear Mop outside! Sammy and Kenny must have come here!"

She ran to open the door.

Mop was there, all right ... but not with the boys. Just one soaking wet dog.

Half of his chewed-off red leash dragged next to him.

Rain dripped from his ears. Water ran down his legs. Puddles formed around his paws.

Dave said what they all were thinking. "Mop's alone! Sammy and Kenny are in some kind of trouble!"

Chapter 12:
Don't Go, Sammy!

At first Kenny and Sammy had played outside in the warm rain.

They stamped in puddles and splashed each other.

Kenny had a flashlight.

They took turns flashing it at each other in Morse code.

They they noticed some flooded-out worms lying on the sidewalk.

Sammy said, "Those poor guys breathe through their skins. They drown if the dirt gets too wet. That's why they come onto the sidewalk."

He fished a couple of worms out of a puddle. "I HATE for anything to die before it has to."

The boys jumped over a river of water that rushed along the curb.

They followed it to a deep puddle over a gutter.

They hunted up branches to use as rakes.

They scratched away a pan cake of leaves that blocked the gutter.

They watched the water suddenly

spin down with a sucking noise.

Then Kenny said, "Hey, let's go over to Dr. Stein's! He invited us!"

Sammy said, "Sure! That's right. To see his computer. Let's go!"

But they were in for a big surprise. When Sammy rang Dr. Stein's bell, Peter opened the door.

He growled, "What are you doing here, fatso?"

Sammy's face burned red. Pulling Mop along, he pushed right past Peter and stamped into the house. Kenny followed him in.

Sammy said, "Dr. Stein invited us! And here we are! Where is he?"

Peter said, "Well, you're out of luck. He's working in his lab. He doesn't want to be bothered. He told us to look for the coins."

Sammy said, "US? You and who

else?" He looked across the room. He saw a teenager sorting through shelves at the back of the room.

A screen stood in front of the lab door.

Peter said, "You might as well get out of here. He won't be done for hours."

Sammy said, "We will wait. We can search for the coins, too, you know."

Mop made a few sniffing noises at Peter's leg.

Peter growled, "Get that ugly wet rat of a dog out of here."

Sammy growled back, "Mop would RATHER be outside, if YOU'RE in here. I'll tie his leash out there. But I bet Dr. Stein will invite him back in."

Peter called to his friend, "Tell the other guys these kids are here."

Sammy said, "Other guys? What other guys?"

Peter said, "I've got two friends searching in the bedroom, too."

Sammy said, "The bedroom? Dr. Stein didn't say to look there!"

Peter laughed. "The old clown doesn't know WHAT room the coins are in."

Sammy looked ready to explode.

He said, "He's no clown. Don't call him that!"

Kenny whispered, "Cool it, Sammy.

They could throw us out."

Sammy seemed to calm down. But inside he was MAD. He decided to pester Peter as much as he could.

Pestering was Sammy's main hobby. He was an expert at it.

So he began searching the shelves right around Peter's feet.

He bumped into Peter's ankles.

He opened a drawer into his shins.

Every few minutes he nagged, "Go tell Dr. Stein we are here, Peter."

Just as Kenny left for the bathroom, Sammy thought of his greatest pestering idea of all time ... his MASTERPIECE.

He pointed to the four huge cans of powdered iced tea mix. He said, "Hey! Maybe the coins are in those!"

Peter fell for it! He ran over to one giant can. He emptied it. He dumped iced tea mix into every pot in the kitchen. But the coins weren't in the can.

Sammy was having a wonderful time. He even forgot that Mop was probably chewing up his leash. Mop always did that when he was tied up.

Sammy said, "You better try the other cans, Peter. Just pour each one into the one that's empty.

"Those cans weigh a TON.

"Just a minute. I'll do it. But, boy, I'm getting thirsty."

Sammy filled a plastic pitcher with water. He set it on the counter.

In a friendly voice he said, "I'll do the cans before I drink anything."

He climbed onto the counter. He pulled off the lids of the three cans.

Then ... he slipped. Anyway, it looked as if he slipped.

All three cans and the pitcher of water spilled onto Peter's legs.

WHAT A MESS! Peter kicked off his shoes.

His pants were covered with wet, gummy sugar-and-tea goo.

Peter's friend looked at the mess. He whispered, "Why don't you just kick those kids out of here?"

Peter hissed, "I can't. Are you kidding? They will just come back with the rest of their dorky friends. Besides, I have a better plan ... "

He ran into the bedroom. He put on a pair of Dr. Stein's pants.

They bunched up around his waist and dragged on the floor.

He rolled up the legs and called his friends around him.

He said, "That's the last straw. That kid out there has got to go. I'm going to lock him and his friend in the lab, like I did good old Unc."

While all this was going on, Kenny had been in the bathroom.

When he came out, he saw that Peter had his back to him. Out of the corner of his eye he saw a mirror across the room. And he saw Peter's face in it.

One of Peter's friends said, "Careful what you say. The other kid's right behind you."

Peter said, "Don't worry. He's deaf, just like Uncle Frank. It's safe."

He went on. "Those two little creeps won't even know they're locked in ... till it's too late. They just want to see the great scientist.

"Some scientist! Doesn't even know he's locked into his own lab. And even if he finds out, he can't get help. No phone in there. I checked."

Kenny COULD hear some of the words Peter was saying.

Sneaking looks in the mirror across the room, he had figured out "... locked in lab ... can't get help ... no phone."

Then Peter called to Sammy, "I think my uncle might let you in now."

He stepped behind the screen in front of the lab door.

Kenny hurried to Sammy and whispered, "Peter has Dr. Stein locked in the lab.

"He put that screen there so we couldn't see the lock was on the door!"

Peter called, "Come on, boys. Unc

says he wants to see you now."

Kenny whispered, "Don't go, Sammy! Peter will lock us in, too!"

Sammy said, "But we have to make sure Dr. Stein is all right! Come on!"

He grabbed Kenny's hand and pulled him into the lab.

The door slammed shut behind them.

Chapter 13: Prisoners

Dr. Stein was at his computer.

He didn't look up when the lab door slammed.

Sammy and Kenny jumped!

Sammy touched Dr. Stein's arm and asked, "Are you all right?"

Dr. Stein said, "Why, Sammy! And Kenny! What a fine surprise!

"Of course I'm all right. Why wouldn't I be?

"And how did you get in? I must not have seen the doorbell light. Anyway, I'm glad you let yourselves in."

Sammy said, "Peter let us in! Didn't you know he was here? With some other guys? Kenny heard him say he locked you in the lab!"

Dr. Stein said, "No! In my own lab? Kenny's hearing aid must have mixed things up!"

Sammy said, "Then you didn't know! Peter is searching your place. I think he wants your coins for himself."

Dr. Stein said, "Come on, my boy. Peter wouldn't steal from me."

He got up as he spoke. He walked to the door. He tried to open it. It didn't move. He shook it. It wouldn't open.

He shook his head sadly. "Kenny heard quite right. We ARE locked in."

His lips pressed together. Deep wrinkles formed around his mouth. His bushy eyebrows met in a terrible frown.

Sammy said, "Dr. Stein, are you OK? You look different all of a sudden."

The doctor exclaimed, "I AM different. I'm MAD!

"Peter's not getting those coins! We shall stop him! Right now!"

Sammy looked around the lab.

He said, "But we can't get out. There aren't any windows. And there isn't a phone, either. And we never told anybody we were coming here."

Dr. Stein said, "Don't you worry. It's PETER who should be worrying!

"I'll show you a REAL MAD SCIENTIST in action!

"Kenny, come over here and see what a computer can do!"

Dr. Stein typed out a message. Then he had Kenny push some computer keys, and the message was sent.

A few minutes later, back at the Woodlanders' house, Dave answered the phone. A scientist in North Dakota was calling.

She read them the message on her computer.

It said: CALL THIS PHONE NUMBER. DR. STEIN AND TWO BOYS LOCKED IN LAB. PETER HOLDING THEM PRISONER. SEND HELP.

Dave called Chief Hemster.

A few minutes later the Woodlanders and the chief were at Dr. Stein's house.

Chief Hemster banged on the door.

Peter opened it. His three big friends stood behind him.

Chief Hemster growled, "Take us to Frank, and FAST."

Peter snapped back, "He doesn't want to be bothered."

Kathy couldn't hold back for one

minute. She said, "Peter, you're a ... a ... LIAR. A TOTAL LIAR."

Chief Hemster looked right at Peter, and he looked MAD.

Peter backed away a few steps. His friends backed away behind him.

The chief backed them all the way to the lab door.

He moved the screen.

Silently Peter turned around and opened the lock.

Sammy came rushing out, with Kenny right behind him.

Sammy hugged Chief Hemster. And he hugged Mrs. Tandy. And he hugged Dave. And he hugged Kathy. And Kenny.

But of course he poked Bill.

Dr. Stein came out. He took a long, sad look at Peter.

Peter called to him, "Come on, Unc!

Tell the police this is just a joke!"

Dr. Stein answered, "This is no joke, Peter. I can't help you out any longer. You're on your own."

Chief Hemster radioed for police cars. Officers came and put Peter and his friends into them.

Peter whined, "I'm crowded back here. I'm uncomfortable."

Chief Hemster said, "Think about how uncomfortable a jail cell might be."

Then the chief went back inside.

He found Sammy saying to Dr. Stein, "I made a terrible mess. I dumped all your powdered tea and some water onto Peter."

Dr. Stein said, "Well, thank goodness you did! Like you said, I would have been drinking that tea for the rest of my life!"

Sammy said, "Well, it's sticky. I

gummed up your floor. But you know, I didn't feel sorry when I was doing it. I guess I really AM a monster."

Dr. Stein said, "You're a wonderful monster! You kept Peter so busy, he didn't find my coins. But it looks like I'LL never find them, either.

"I've looked in every spot in this room. And you searched it. And I bet Peter did many times when I was out.

"The only one who HASN'T searched this place is my plastic man."

Sammy said, "Well, I bet he would, too, except he's probably not feeling so good. You wouldn't, either, if you had an empty space where your liver should be."

And then Dave shouted, "EMPTY SPACE! YOU'VE GOT IT, SAMMY!"

Bill yelled, "EMPTY SPACE! HURRAY, SAMMY!"

Kathy said, "SAMMY! YOU'RE WON-DERFUL!"

Mrs. Tandy said, "My great detective!"

Dr. Stein grinned and said, "My dear-est monster! Empty space! That's it!"

Chief Hemster said, "Could some one tell me what you're all talking about?"

Kenny said, "And me?"

Sammy said, "I sure can't. If you want to know what I think ... I think they've all gone bonkers."

But by then the others had dashed over to the plastic man.

Bill lifted off an outer layer of plastic muscles.

Dave removed an inner muscle wall.

And from where the liver should have been, out fell three bags of coins ... clink ... clink ... clink ... onto the floor.

Bill grabbed the plastic man and danced around the room with him.

Mrs. Tandy, Kenny, Dr. Stein, Sammy, Kathy, and Chief Hemster cheered.

Then Dr. Stein said, "Gather around, everyone! We are having a party!

"And tomorrow I will look into getting a hearing aid ... since Kenny used his to rescue me."

Kenny said, "And I'm going to give computers a chance, since you used yours to rescue US!"

Dr. Stein rushed to the cupboard. He took out a huge cookie jar. He said, "Here, everybody. Cookies! And thanks to Sammy, we don't have to drink tea."

He poured milk for them.

Then he said, "Sammy and Kenny, I want you to always remember how brave you were tonight. So I have a gift for each of you."

Carefully he placed something small in each boy's hand.

When they looked down, they could hardly believe what they saw.

In Kenny's hand lay the wonderful monkey carved from a peach pit.

And in Sammy's hand lay the beautiful copper coin.